Walkers

A One Act Play for Four Actresses

by

Patricia Rockwell

Production Rights: Amateur groups may produce this play without royalty payment if they purchase five copies of the script. Please send production photos to: cozycapress@gmail.com

For information, visit our website at: www.cozycatpress.com

COZY CAT
P R E S S

ISBN: 978-1-952579-49-3

Printed in the United States of America

10 9 8 7 6 5 4 3 2 1

Dedicated to my Mom, the original Essie.

Walkers

(Scene: An all-purpose room. Four women enter, each pushing a walker. There is a card table C.)

Essie: Well, ladies, it looks like we have the all-purpose room to ourselves. (She moves DS to an imaginary full-length mirror located in fourth wall). Oh, Bev did a good job on my hair.

Opal: (Helping Fay get settled at table) I'll put your walker over here by the wall, Fay. (She does so). Essie, your hair is always so shiny.

Marjorie: (Putting her purse at table and joining Essie DS). Now, Essie, if you'd just *wear* something more befitting your lovely hair...

Essie: What do you mean by that, Marjorie?

Marjorie: Isn't this the fourth day in a row you've had on those dowdy old pants and that over-sized tunic?

Essie: My clothes are clean—that's what counts. And I'll have you know I never wear a top more than two days or trousers more than...well, not too often.

Opal: (joining them) That's all right, Essie. Your wardrobe is one of convenience rather than style. Come on, ladies. Let's play cards. Fay is anxious to get started. (They all stare at Fay.)

Marjorie: Fay is almost asleep in her chair, Opal. She doesn't look all that anxious. (They roll their walkers back to the table and sit.)

Essie: Purple potholders, Marjorie! Why would I need to be *stylish* at Happy Haven? I'm a ninety-year-old woman. I'm not trying to impress anyone.

Opal: That's true, Marjorie. Essie's not chasing after men like you are.

Marjorie: Don't be ridiculous, Opal. I don't *need* to chase after men. *They* chase after me.

Essie: Of course they do. (Rolling her eyes)

Marjorie: Probably because *I* don't wear the same outfit every day.

Opal: Marjorie, you're just asking for trouble. Canasta time now, girls! Who wants to deal?

Marjorie: I will. (She grabs cards, shuffles and deals them to women. She leaves remaining cards in the center of table with one card set aside as a discard pile. They start game.)

Essie: For your information, I went through my closet the other day to find things to donate to charity. I couldn't believe how much junk I'd accumulated. I had no idea what a lot of clothes I had. Over two dozen brassieres. Can you believe that?

Marjorie: I have that many if not more. I have some to wear with sweaters, some for backless gowns, some black, some white. I mean, a girl needs a whole variety of bras.

Essie: Maybe you do, Marjorie. You probably need a different bra for each man you have your eyes on. But for me, one or two are plenty.

Opal: So what did you do with your left-over bras, Essie?

Essie: Well, I didn't save them for Marjorie, that's for sure!

Marjorie: Good, because they wouldn't fit! (She juts out her bosom dramatically.) Your bras would be far too *small* for me, Essie!

Opal: Marjorie!

Essie: Oh, don't worry, Opal. She doesn't bother me. I don't want her big boobs.

Opal: Ladies, please! Can we get back to our game? (They concentrate on the card game.)

Essie: It's so much nicer playing Canasta in this all-purpose room when those yoga people aren't grunting and groaning all over the place.

Marjorie: I rather enjoy yoga class, especially when some of the men at Happy Haven attend.

Essie: You would. You'd like taking out the garbage as long as a man accompanied you.

Opal: (snickering) Well, she didn't like being in that upside down yoga pose the other day when Edgar Buckley poked her in the posterior.

Marjorie: (giggling) Oh, that man! He's terrible. I almost peed my pants!

Opal: Really, Marjorie? I can't imagine anything would make *your* bladder malfunction.

Essie: Why would you say that, Opal? At our age just about anything can cause—as you say—a bladder malfunction. (She plays a card.)

Marjorie: Maybe for you, Essie, but Opal's right. I pride myself on controlling my bladder. It takes a lot to make me tinkle. And Edgar almost did. (She discards.) Fay, it's your turn! (Fay awakens, glances at her cards, then adds to the discard pile.) Fay discarded. Play, Opal!

Opal: I'm thinking.

Essie: Marjorie, do you really think you can *control* your bladder?

Marjorie: Essie, you'd be surprised what body parts *I* can control! (She wiggles her shoulders.)

Opal: Marjorie! Do we have to discuss *body parts* at the card table? (She plays a card.) People outside might hear. (She glances around the room.)

Essie: No one's listening to us in here. They're all watching *Wheel of Fortune* in the TV room.

Marjorie: So what if I discuss my body, Opal? Are you a prude? (She leans over the table and playfully pokes Opal on the nose.)

Opal: No! (pushing away her hand). Stop that! It's just unseemly.

Essie: I don't know, Opal. Marjorie could provide us a service. I mean, I'd like to hear her advice on bladder control. I admit that my bladder—um—has a mind of its own.

Marjorie: We *know*, Essie. You've let us know more than once about your...bladder issues.

Opal: And, we've suggested over and over that the answer is simple. Just use those adult—

Essie: Don't even say it, Opal! (She slaps the table.) If there's one thing I will *not* do, it's wear those infantile (whispering) *diapers*. I'm an adult, not a baby. As long as I can *walk* to a bathroom, that's what I'm going to do. I mean, would either of *you* wear them?

Opal: Of course not!

Marjorie: Never!

Essie: I rest my case.

Marjorie: But, of course, Opal and I *are* younger than you, Essie.

Essie: Only by a few years.
Opal: I'm sure Fay wears them. (She nods to Fay who has dozed off again.)

Marjorie: She *must* wear them. I mean, she just sits around all day. Her aide probably puts them on her in the morning. You're with her most of the day, Opal. Don't you know?

Opal: No. I don't. Fay isn't very…disclosive. I don't know

all that much about her really. Other than that before she came here, she was a librarian, so she must have been able to speak at one time. Nobody here really knows when or why she became mute. They say something happened to her late in her life before she arrived at Happy Haven that caused her to quit talking. I've never heard her say a word. (The three companions all glance over at Fay.)

Marjorie: You could check.

Opal: What? That's disgusting, Marjorie!

Essie: Stop it, you two! It doesn't matter what Fay wears or doesn't wear in the panty department. I'm more interested in what Marjorie *does*. I mean, you say you can control your bladder. If that's true, I'd really like to know *how* you do it. Your technique, that is.

Opal: Marjorie, if Essie could control her bladder, she could come on field trips with us.

Essie: No! That wasn't what I meant. I just want to be able to have better bladder control. Anyone would. What does that have to do with field trips?

Marjorie: Essie, you always refuse to go with us on Happy Haven field trips. You miss out on some fantastic places. You always say it's because you won't be able to find a restroom.

Essie: I won't.

Opal: We rest our case. Field trips, bladder control. They go together. At least for you, Essie.

Essie: Oh, fiddling fiddlesticks! (She slumps back in her chair.)

Opal: Essie, you're the bravest woman I know. I can't believe you—of all people—are frightened of a little panty accident.

Essie: I'm not frightened. (Marjorie and Opal put down their cards abruptly. Fay dozes.)

Opal: Then what is it?

Essie: Okay, I'm frightened.

Marjorie: Booooo! (She raises her hands and does a "scary face" to frighten Essie.)

Essie: Stop it, Marjorie! Just teach me your trick for maintaining good bladder control.

Marjorie: Okay, I will, Essie. The secret is—Kegels!

Essie: Kugels? Aren't those German coffee cakes?

Marjorie: No! Kegels are exercises. *And* you'll be happy to know there are *other* benefits to doing them besides just bladder control. (She wiggles her eyebrows suggestively.)

Essie: I don't want to know your *other* benefits, Marjorie, although I can guess. I just want to live my life—with dry pants. I may be over ninety, but I'm not ready for the junk heap yet. You know, I rebelled when I first had to use my walker, but once I saw how much faster I could move with it and how much easier it made it to get around, I was a convert. Now, my walker is just like an extension of my legs. It makes me feel like I'm one of those "bionic" women. (She rises and demonstrates how fast she can move with her walker.) See!

Opal: That's enough, Essie. Come back here and play your cards!

Essie: (sits back down and plays a card) I heard that Bob Weiderly is in the hospital. Someone said he collapsed after bingo last night.

Marjorie: I know. You have a crush on Bob, don't you, Essie?

Essie: Merciful marshmallows, Marjorie! I do not. I'm too old for him. He's only 82.

Opal: Have you noticed how men seem to win Bingo games here more often than women?

Essie: What? That's impossible! First of all, there's no way men could ever do anything more *often* than women here at Happy Haven because we outnumber them...

Opal and Marjorie: Eight to one!

Marjorie: Yes, Essie, we know. The odds are terrible for us women.

Opal: Bob Weiderly is full of himself. When he wins, he claims his prize like an Olympic medal.

Essie: Sibilant sassafras! Opal, if my memory serves me...

Opal: And it hardly ever does...

Essie: If my memory serves me correctly, Opal, you won Bingo last week and when you collected that dollar bill as a prize, you'd think they'd just crowned you Miss America!

Marjorie: Technically, Opal *is* the only one among us who could *qualify* for the *Miss* America contest because it's for *unmarried* women only, and we all know that Opal is a *spinster*. Most Happy Haven women are widows. I *myself* have had several husbands and numerous boyfriends. (Marjorie flings her arms out and bows. Fay responds by smiling and clapping)

Essie: Marjorie, quit showing off your figure!

Marjorie: At least I *have* a figure, Essie!

Opal: You're both being ridiculous.

Marjorie: Does Bob have heart trouble?

Essie: Everybody has heart trouble at our age.

Opal: I don't. My heart is in excellent condition, according to my cardiologist.

Marjorie: If your heart's in excellent condition, why do you need a cardiologist? (Opal huffs.)

Essie: I'm healthy as a horse.

Opal: I've known some pretty sickly horses in my day, Essie. I grew up on a farm.

Essie: What I meant to say is that my geroto—my geron—my gerotono—you know what I mean. My old person's doctor says I'm a healthy old person!

Opal: What about your memory? You always forget what you ate the very next day.

Essie: So? Who cares if I remember what I eat? That's not important. What's important is that I remember to take my pills—and I do.

Opal: You mean your *aide* remembers for you.

Marjorie: Oh, it could be important to remember what you eat, Essie. I mean, just imagine if you weren't supposed to eat something you were allergic to—like Brussel sprouts—and you forgot if you ate it or not.

Essie: Blubbering blueberries! First of all, I wouldn't eat Brussel sprouts because they're icky. And why would I eat Brussel sprouts if I was allergic to them? You two are ridiculous. Fay, you have the right idea. Just sleep through the game! (Fay opens one eye when she hears her name and claps.)

Opal: Why is *she* so chatty all of a sudden?

Marjorie: Who knows?

Essie: Bob always seemed so healthy. He uses a cane, but have you *seen* him at exercise class?

Marjorie: You mean, have I seen him in his gym shorts? He does have a nice physique.

Essie: He can do more push-ups than any other man at Happy Haven.

Opal: That wouldn't be much of a challenge.

Essie: The point is—if you'll let me finish—Bob is probably in better health than most...

Marjorie: He *is* a fine specimen of manhood. (She shimmies her shoulders suggestively.)

Opal: Really, Essie. At age 82, a man can have a heart attack just *because*.

Marjorie: Maybe he collapsed because he was having sex.

Opal: Marjorie! What would make you suggest that?

Marjorie: It's a possibility. I wouldn't kick him out of bed for eating crackers! (Suddenly, Fay places some cards in her hand neatly on the various columns in front of her and claps.)

Opal: Look! Fay just melded! I didn't even think she was paying attention.

Marjorie: You sly minx, Fay. (Marjorie pinches Fay's cheek.) You really know your Canasta!

Essie: Don't underestimate Fay. You never know what she might be up to. Good job, Fay.

Intercom Announcer: Good morning, Happy Haven residents! (The women return to their game.) Don't forget to sign up for our botanical gardens field trip. Remember, the gardens have some of the most exquisite indigenous flowering plants in our area. We still have room for four more participants. Just add your name to the sign-up sheet at the front desk. Buses leave for the gardens this Thursday at 10:30 a.m.

Marjorie: You should go on that trip, Essie. You love gardening.

Essie: Not someone else's gardening. And besides, I hate field trips. You know that.

Marjorie: You mean you hate being too far from a bathroom.

Essie: There's never a toilet around when you need one.

Opal: Some of those big buses have toilets. Not the Happy Haven bus, of course.

Essie: I would never use a toilet on a bus. What do you take me for? Some kind of hippie? There's probably graffiti all over the walls. I will have to admit, though, that thinking about those botanical gardens really gets my juices flowing.

Marjorie: Which juices would those be?

Essie: Not *those* juices, Marjorie. Get your mind out of the gutter.

Marjorie: It wasn't in the gutter; it was in the bedroom.

Essie: I meant my...creative juices. Reminds me of my flower growing days.

Marjorie: Fay, it's your turn! (Marjorie nudges Fay who shakes herself and looks at the cards on the table. Then, she places all the cards in her hand on the columns in front of her.)

Opal: What! She just went out! We barely started playing!

Marjorie: How did you do that, Fay? (She rises and rolls behind Fay, examining Fay's cards.)

Essie: I don't believe it. No, I take that back. Actually, now, I'll believe anything.

Intercom: Residents! Don't forget that after dinner tonight, our favorite ventriloquist Geoffrey George will be here with his pals Ducky and Doozy to perform for you in the lobby. You won't want to miss the fun. Seven sharp. And, don't forget to sign up for the field trip to the botanical gardens at the front desk. Only four slots left. We hear the roses are in bloom. Also, anyone who might have seen Agnes Woolwhistle's gold-handled cane, please report to the front desk.

Essie: Heavens to hollyhocks! Agnes Woolwhistle is always losing her cane. Someone ought to tie it around her neck. (The women start another hand of cards.)

Opal: Speaking of losing things, Hubert Darby's suspenders fell off again yesterday. Will that man ever learn to keep his pants up?

Marjorie: You're right. Whenever he bends over, you can see his crack.

Opal: Marjorie!

Marjorie: You've heard worse, Opal. First graders say 'butt crack' all the time. It's one of their favorite insults.

Opal: We're not first graders.

Essie: Stop it, you two! The poor man probably doesn't have a clue his pants are drooping.

Marjorie: I don't care if his pants fall down. It's fine with me. More men should wear suspenders and then maybe more pants would drop.

Opal: Marjorie, you're disgusting!

Essie: I'm sure his suspenders will do their job, ladies. Hubert Darby doesn't deserve this kind of treatment from either of you.

Marjorie: I know why you're defending him, Essie. Hubert is smitten with you. I think he wears those red suspenders to make you happy. He's probably planning to plight his troth to you.

Opal: He should be certain his suspenders are hooked to his pants before he goes courting.

Essie: Hubert Darby is not smitten with me. I'm just—someone he confides in.

Marjorie: It's more than that, Essie. You'll see. I know the signs. I used to see this kind of behavior in many a love-struck first-grade boy when I taught elementary school.

Essie: Look! Fay's nodded off again. Was it something we

said, Fay? (When her name is mentioned, Fay wakens abruptly, gives a puzzled smile and nods off again.) Oh, guess what? I got one of those answering machines today! My daughters insisted I have one. (She scowls).

Marjorie: They think you're senile.

Opal: The answering machine is their way of keeping track you.

Marjorie: I have an answering machine.

Opal: Me too.

Essie: So we're all senile?

Opal: Actually, I think you'll love your answering machine, Essie. There have been times when I was expecting an important phone call and I simply didn't want to leave my apartment because I was afraid I'd miss it. With an answering machine, you can just go about your business and when you come back, that little red light is there—blinking—letting you know that someone has called. It's very reassuring. (She thinks a bit.) Or frightening.

Essie: It has a lot of buttons. I hate buttons. My television remote has buttons. My telephone has buttons. Every time I get some new machine, it seems to have more buttons than before. I've seen all the buttons on those fancy cell phones my daughters use. And I don't even want to think about computers. I don't get all this technology. So many buttons. I like things simple. I *think* better when the world is simple.

Marjorie: Oh, Essie, you'll get used to your answering machine. Actually, I agree with Opal. It's so much fun to come back to my room and find that little red light blinking away.

Essie: I can understand *you* liking red lights, Marjorie, but Opal?

Opal: I really do like the little red light, Essie. It lets you know people are thinking of you.

Essie: Like the cemetery plot salesman. (pause) Oh, all right. Maybe I'll give it a try.

Opal: Now you sound like the Essie I know and love.

Marjorie: You sound like the Essie I know and love too.

Essie: Thank you, girls. I do feel better having your support. (More card playing.)

Opal: Your hair looks wonderful today, Essie.

Essie: Thank you, Opal. Bev always does it just to my liking.

Marjorie: You have beautiful hair, Essie. It's so shiny and full. How does Bev do it?

Essie: I don't know. She washes it. She curls it.

Opal: You were blessed with good hair genes, Essie. I wish my hair was like yours. Mine is so thin and lifeless. There's not much Bev can do to help it. She tries though, bless her heart.

Essie: Well, thank you, Opal. I don't see anything wrong with your hair. I'm always amazed how you manage to wrap it in such an intricate fashion the way you do each day.

Opal: I've always had long hair and I learned how to put it in a bun years ago. Of course, nowadays, my morning aide helps me some, because my arthritis is so bad in my fingers.

Marjorie: That's the benefit of short hair, Opal. Like mine.

Essie: Your hair is such a lovely color, Marjorie.

Marjorie: Isn't it? It's Color Essence Number 32—Silky Fox.

Opal: What?

Marjorie: That's the hair color shade I use. You didn't think that I was a natural redhead, did you?

Essie: I don't know. Why not?

Marjorie: I have no problem assisting Mother Nature in *all* areas—not just my hair color. (She winks.)

Opal: You mean…?

Marjorie: It's true. I'm not a natural 36D. Don't tell anyone. (She juts out her breasts again.)

Essie: Marjorie, you can do whatever you like to enhance your looks, but I just don't see why you'd bother. At our age, what good does it do to fight against the inevitable?

Marjorie: What good? Essie, you may not care about it, but *I* would like to attract a man!

And there are precious few of them here at Happy Haven. After all, the ratio of men to women is only (All except Fay say, "8 to 1") And, Essie, you might not have noticed, but I'm not the *only* female resident at Happy Haven who uses certain enhancements to improve her looks.

Opal: I don't.

Marjorie: That's your prerogative, Opal.

Opal: I agree with Essie. We're too old to be dyeing our hair and enhancing our breasts.

Marjorie: Speak for yourself, Opal! And remember, I'm the *youngest* of the four of us.

Essie: We don't know that for certain. You might *not* be the youngest. Remember, there's Fay. (Essie nods across the table to Fay. All stare at her. Fay slowly looks around and smiles).

Marjorie: We don't know how old Fay is.

Opal: She's probably younger than all of us. (Fay smiles)

Essie: Or older. (Fay frowns.)

Marjorie: We'll never know, because she'll never tell.

Opal: She does use the computer. She could send us her age in one of those x-mails.

Marjorie: You mean e-mails.

Opal: Whatever. Actually, she's very good at computers. No wonder she's good at Canasta.

Essie: Computers are like big giant monsters to me. They scare me.

Marjorie: Me too.

Opal: I can use computers a bit. I had to when I was an executive assistant, but it was mostly just word processing.

Essie: That's better than me, Opal. I never processed a word in my life. Maybe a sausage or two. (pause, they play more cards.)

Marjorie: What did you all think of the dance the men did the other day in the dining hall? Oh, my! Wasn't that fabulous? Didn't you love it, Opal?

Opal: I thought it was energetic, but not terribly appropriate for senior citizens.

Marjorie: I love to see men move their hips.

Essie: Not everyone is as open-minded as you, Marjorie.

Marjorie: That's true. What did you think, Fay? (Fay giggles and smiles). See, she liked it!

Opal: It *was* a catchy tune. That Upside Down Funk song or whatever it was called.

Essie: I was surprised when the men just popped up all over the dining hall and started dancing.

Marjorie: It's called a flash mob. They do them in shopping malls, airports, all sorts of places.

Opal: But how do they prepare them? I mean, they must have to rehearse, don't they?

Marjorie: True. They must have practiced somewhere.

Essie: All of them? That dance must have included all the men at Happy Haven. I don't see how they could have gotten all of them together in one spot at one time to practice.

Opal: Yes. Just when would they have done that?

Marjorie: Well, they did! And there aren't *that* many men here anyway. You know women outnumber men (All the women except Fay say "8 to 1"), so it would be easier to gather the men together than the women. (Fay is tapping her hands on the arms of her chair and nodding her head back and forth in time to an imaginary song.)

Essie: Well, one thing we know. Fay must have enjoyed the dance. She may not talk, but she's obviously not deaf.

Opal: I don't know, Essie. A deaf person would have heard *that* music!

Marjorie: When they started dancing, I wanted to run out there and kiss every man on the floor!

Essie: I'm surprised you didn't.

Marjorie: I'm a very passionate person, Essie, and like to demonstrate my affection in public.

Opal: Yes, we've come to know that about you. How many husbands did you have again?

Marjorie: I had two, Opal; you know that. Maybe a boyfriend or two—*before, between*, and *after* the husbands, of course.

Essie: Not *during*?

Marjorie: Essie! What do you take me for? Some kind of hussy?

Essie: Your word, Marjorie. (Fay giggles. They look at her. Fay picks up and stares at cards.)

Marjorie: I'm just very passionate.

Essie: I don't care if you canoodle with every man at Happy Haven, Marjorie.

Opal: Essie! *Canoodle!* How could you use such a word?

Essie: What's wrong with *canoodle*? I thought it meant hugging and kissing.

Opal: I think it means *more* than that.

Marjorie: Well, I know I'd like to canoodle the pants off Fred Morgan.

Opal: You're welcome to him.

Essie: Really, Opal? So why do you *blush* every time his name is mentioned?

Opal: I do not. (Opal blushes.)

Essie: I rest my case. Look at her face.

Opal: I can't help it. Blushing's a neurological reaction. It has nothing to do with Fred—Mr. Morgan.

Marjorie: Oh, it's Fred now.

Opal: Will you two stop it?

Essie: I'm sorry, Opal.

Marjorie: I'm not. Opal's always so prim and proper. I like to see her girly-girly over some man.

Opal: I'm just not *used* to seeing men gyrating around like that. It must be that *awful* dance.

Essie: You mean, the upside down funky? Or whatever it was?

Opal: Yes, that thing! Now I can't even think of Fred—I mean Mr. Morgan—without seeing him up there gyrating his hips about like some low-life Hollywood stripper.

Marjorie: And what's so bad about that?

Opal: It's just not the image I had of him. He was always such a sweet, gentle man. So soft-spoken and considerate. Seeing him dance like that—well—it made me uncomfortable.

Marjorie: Really, Opal, if the poor man can't break out and have a little fun at his age when can he? I mean, we're in a retirement home—not a jail.

Essie: I agree with Marjorie on this, Opal. I'm sure your Mr. Morgan is a lovely gentleman. You mustn't judge him too harshly. What's wrong with him letting his hair down a little? He certainly appeared to be having a good time while he was dancing. You said once that after his wife died he lost interest in life. Well, maybe dancing has given him that interest back. Or—maybe it was seeing *you* respond to that dance that has given him that interest back.

Opal: I don't know....

Marjorie: Come on, Opal, give him a chance. You two can canoodle the night away.

Opal: I...I'll think about it.

Marjorie: Well, don't think too long or I'll take him.

Opal: You can't have every man at Happy Haven, Marjorie!

Marjorie: Me? I don't have *any* man at Happy Haven. Everyone has someone, *except* me. Essie has Bob, Opal has Fred, Fay will probably start dating the UPS man and where will I be?

Essie: You'll be where we all are. Single. Just like we were yesterday and the day before. I'm perfectly happy that way. We're not a bunch of teenage girls fighting over the football quarterback. We're mature women. We don't fight over men.

Marjorie: Maybe you don't, Essie, but I do when I see my fellow tablemates snapping up all the eligible ones.

Opal: No one is snapping up anybody.

Essie: Well, Marjorie, if you're *truly* desperate, I guess you could have Hank.

Opal: Hank? The Happy Haven plumber?

Essie: He seems available. I've gotten to know him recently while he's been fixing my toilet.

Opal: Oh, You have a broken toilet? Then, it's good you got him—*on* it, right away.

Essie: Yes, speed is important with toilet repair. You can't just sit around and let it go to *pot*.

Marjorie: No, before you know it, everything might get *flushed* away. (She giggles.)

Essie: Although I'll admit that after waiting so long for him to fix it, I was quite *pooped*. (All three women except Fay are giggling uproariously now.)

Marjorie: (when the laughter subsides) Do you have anything to eat, Essie? I'm hungry.

Essie: Let me check in my walker. (opening seat on her walker). You know, I believe I do. (She pulls out a cellophane bag of candies). Here are some chocolates I got as a prize for a crossword puzzle contest I won a while back.

Opal: You won a contest? You mean one here at Happy Haven?

Essie: No. It was something I found inside one of my crossword puzzle books and I entered it and I won these candies. I don't really care that much for candy, so I put them in my walker seat and forgot about them. You might as well have them.

Marjorie: Since when do you enter contests, Essie? Ooo, these look yummy! (Marjorie selects one of the chocolates and takes a dainty bite.) Wow! This is fabulous! It's much better than that dry kind they normally hand out in the dining room after meals.

Opal: Oh, give me one. (She rises from her chair and rolls walker over to Marjorie. Marjorie holds out the sack to Opal, who examines the chocolates and selects one. She takes a bite and rolls back to her chair.) This is good. Yum. It's called "A-ma-ret-to." That means *love*.

Marjorie: Ooo, it *is* tasty. I think I'll have another one.

Opal: Don't hog them all, Marjorie. Give me another. You've had two already. (Marjorie bends over the table, and Opal reaches for it but she

can't reach the sack. The two
women laugh.)

Essie: What's wrong with you
two? You're being ridiculous.

Opal: You're the ridiculous one.
(Opal gets up and plods her
walker over to Marjorie for
another chocolate. She grabs
one and turns to go, then
reaches back and grabs a
second one. Taking a big bite
out of one, she looks at the
interior) Ooo! This one's
"Creme de mint." I love mint.
(She nestles back down into her
arm chair and lifts one leg over
the arm rest.)

Essie: Opal! Put your leg down. I
can see your underpants. What
is wrong with you?

Opal: Nothing. I'm just relaxing.
These candies are delish. Ooo!

Marjorie! Look at this one. It's caramel. (She takes a nibble from her third chocolate and a very runny caramel oozes out. Laughing, Opal slurps up the liquid as some of it dribbles onto her sweater.)

Marjorie: He he! Opal is a slob! Opal is a slob! (She points at the mess Opal is making. Marjorie gobbles up her third chocolate without spilling. Opal and Marjorie are now laughing loudly.)

Essie: What is wrong with you two? Fay, are you seeing this? (Essie looks at Fay who is glancing back and forth between Marjorie and Opal, her eyes wide open.)

Opal: Let Fay have a candy, Essie. (The bag is passed to Fay who cautiously takes one, unwraps it and nibbles it.)

Essie: Give me one of those. (The women hand a candy to Essie. She unwraps it, smells it, and takes a small bite.) Oh, galloping galoshes! I know what it is! (She rises out of her chair and rolls her walker over to Marjorie. She grabs the sack of chocolates from Marjorie's hands.) Give me that bag!

Marjorie: Essie! You said we could eat them.

Essie: That was before I realized what was in them. (She turns the bag over and reads the side.) Just as I thought! Every one of these little devils contains *alcohol*. Or as it's phrased on the ingredients label—*liqueur*. You're both drunk—Opal evidently more so than you, Marjorie. (She tosses the bag in the waste basket.) That's enough for you both! Now what do we do?

Marjorie: We'll be fine, Essie. (She stretches out in her chair) I can hold my liquor. I only had a few sips—or bites—or whatever. (She giggles.) I can't speak for Opal.

Opal: I am so fine! Oh, *so* fine. (She slurs her words, both legs draped over edge of the chair.)

Essie: You are *not* fine, Opal! Come on, both of you. Get up! (Essie forces them both up.)

Opal: Why? Am I an alcoholic? I'm so comfy here. These are the best arm chairs. I could sleep on these chairs. (She stretches her body out so her head is draped over one arm of the chair.)

Essie: Get up, Opal! You're going to walk this off now. (Essie pulls, unsuccessfully, on Opal's legs in an attempt to place them on the ground in a more lady-like pose.) Stand up, Opal!

Marjorie: I'll help you, Essie. Come on, Opal! Let's march! (Marjorie starts marching around in time to an unheard beat. Fay stares at her friends and slowly nibbles on her chocolate.)

Essie: Opal, get up this instant! Fay, don't eat that! (She give one last pull which dethrones Opal from her seat, launching the two women backwards and both onto the floor.)

Opal: Here at Happy Haven, we're all just one big happy family, aren't we, Essie? That's why we call it *Happy* Haven. If I go into detox will you come visit me, Essie? I've never had alcohol before. It tastes so good. I'm so happy! (She flings her arms around Essie.) I love you, Essie! I could sleep right here on the floor. You can sleep here beside me, Essie.

Essie: (on floor, to self). My John always told me that I was my loveliest when I was asleep. I thought he meant I looked like sleeping beauty, but I think he meant that I wasn't talking.

Opal: (on the floor) Maybe I'll just go to sleep right here and Prince Charming will come along and wake me with a kiss.

Essie: No, Opal. We need to get you off the floor. Give me a hand, Marjorie. (Marjorie dances over and only partially helps Essie raise Opal to a standing position.) Stop it, Marjorie! This isn't helping.

Marjorie: I wasn't trying to help; I was trying to get Opal's goat. (Both Marjorie and Opal explode with laughter. Marjorie lands on floor. Essie is at first furious, then she softens.)

Essie: (on ground, she laughs too) Oh, cackling crocodiles! I love laughing with you all. (She embraces them. Fay claps and rolls herself down to join them on floor.) You know, ladies, people think just because we're old that we're ready for the scrap heap. Well, they're wrong! (She rises.) Just look at us. (She points to the imaginary mirror DS. The others get up.)

Marjorie: We are rather cute, aren't we? Or do we just look cute because we're drunk?

Opal: Cute is not an appropriate term for women our age. (She burps and they all laugh.)

Essie: I'm fine with cute, Opal. I'm fine with whatever Marjorie or any of us wants to call ourselves. I can't help it. When my bladder is empty, I feel like I can conquer the world.

Marjorie: And you look like it too, Essie.

Essie: You know what we really look like? One of those singing sister acts from the 40's.

Marjorie: I know! The Walkers! (She gyrates her walker back and forth and the others follow.)

Essie: When three—I mean *four*— (she takes Fay's arm and they all grab hands) ladies of a certain age—get behind their walkers and put their minds to it—there's no telling what they can do! (The four women dance around using their walkers like a singing group.)

Intercom: Attention, residents! It's time for our monthly emergency fire drill! (The ladies all freak out.) All residents move as quickly as possible to the front lawn! Please don't stop to collect personal items or make last minute trips to the bathroom. Hypothetically, your life could depend on it. Now! Move! The local fire chief is timing our drill! Go! Go! (They attempt to exit, yelling at each other, bumping into each other and falling down.)

THE END